CJ'S BIG DREAM
A STORY BY C.J. WATSON

WRITTEN BY TAMIKA NEWHOUSE
ILLUSTRATED BY CAMERON WILSON

CJ's Big Dream ©2019
C.J. Watson
ISBN: 9781702097260

Published by Quiet Storm Foundation

THIS BOOK IS DEDICATED TO THE LIL' BOY OR LIL' GIRL READING THIS BOOK. MAY YOU FIND INSPIRATION IN THIS STORY TO ACHIEVE YOUR GOALS!
CUE IN ROCKY THEME SONG MUSIC

The sun beams in through the blinds as CJ awakens. "Today's the big day!" He says as he climbs out of his bed. He glances over at his trophies that sit on his dresser and basketball posters on the wall, and boasts, "Today I will get closer to my dreams."

After brushing his teeth, CJ gets dressed for school. Prepared for his day, he takes one last look in the mirror before grabbing his lucky socks off the floor. "These will help me win today's big game for sure!"

His socks are worn and dingy with discoloration from being worn so many times.

That does not matter to CJ however, because each time he wears these socks he wins the big game.

"Ready for the big game?" CJ's mother asks.

CJ beams with joy at his mama as she sits his breakfast down on the table in front of him. The smell of mama's blueberry pancakes, bacon, and eggs makes CJ very excited.

"Ewww, you have on those stinky socks," his younger brother whines.

"These are my lucky socks and they'll help me win today's big game," CJ replies before taking a bite of his pancakes.

His father hands him his book bag. "Have a good day at school son and we'll see you later at the game."

CJ hugs his father goodbye and starts his journey off to school with a stomach full of his mama's blueberry pancakes. He is confident that today will be a great day.

On his way to his new school, CJ see's how bad his neighborhood looks.

Abandoned buildings, old homes with uncut grass, and graffiti were everywhere.

It makes CJ sad to see his neighborhood like this. But his thoughts about the big game make him feel hopeful about his day again.

10

Arriving to his school CJ feels a comfort with the change of scenery.

The sun seems brighter as it shines off the school's landscape. The green grass and the large building gives him a sense of newness.

He sees some of his new friends come up to him. "CJ ready for today? It's going to be a tough game." Tim asks.

"We're going to win today's game. I have these on." He points to his obviously dingy socks and his classmates seem confused.

"You go to school here with us now, I'll make sure you have some new socks for the game. Our star player has to look the best." Tim jokes.

SCHOOL

It's after school and CJ walks into the gym ready for warms-ups and he's excited.

"Ready to shoot some hoops?" Coach Madison calls out to CJ as he walks into the gym.

"Ready as I'll ever be, coach!"

Coach Madison throws CJ a basketball and yells out, "Shoot!"

CJ's standing in the middle of the gym, far away from the basket. "You want me to shoot from here?" He asks, uncertain if he can make it.

"Yes, trust your hands CJ."

He focuses in on the basket and shoots the ball. But misses!

"No!" Feeling ashamed, CJ stomps his feet. "Come on lucky socks, you have to help me win."

Coach calls out to CJ, "Don't think about how far the basket is. Just show me how strong those arms are. Focus on your strength."

CJ grips the ball tightly and bends his knees to shoot the ball. "I can make it. Just focus." He tells himself.

Digging the tips of his toes into the bottom of his shoes, he gives off a huge jump, extends his arms, and pushes the ball out of his hands into the air.

Off it goes...flying into the sky and headed towards the magical square on the backboard.

16

It's game time!

CJ has the ball and is dribbling down the court. You can hear his family cheering from the stands.

"Go CJ go!"

He dribbles to the left, and then dribbles quickly to the right, the other player stumbles and falls. Seeing an opening, CJ zooms pass the other team and he begins to hear his coach's voice in his head.

"Don't think about how far the basket is. Just show me how powerful those arms are. Focus on your strength."

With all of his power, he throws his arms in the air and releases the ball in the air.
The crowd cheers.

"Go, go gooooo!" CJ cheers never taking his eyes off the basketball.

Swoosh!

"And the home team wins!" The referee roars.

"We won!" CJ leaps in the air excitedly.

"You did it son!" CJ's Dad runs up to him and hugs him tightly. "You're on your way to living out your dreams son.

"I just have to keep working hard!" says CJ.

"You're right son, but for now celebrate your win." He pats him on his shoulder and smiles proudly.

"Thanks Dad!"

CJ feels proud of himself.

He looks down at his lucky socks and whispers. "We did it!"

"Now that the game is over, what shall we do now, Son?" His Father asks.

Holding the trophy in his hands, CJ shouts, "I am going to win the next game and the next game and then the very next game Dad. I'll keep winning until I get to the NBA!"

"Is that right?"

"That's right!" CJ says, reassuring his Dad.

"Dreaming big, aren't you?"

"This is only the beginning Dad. I have big dreams." He says as they walk off the court. "Until the next game!"